The Trip
to Panama

Translated by Anthea Bell

BELTZ
&Gelberg

M NI AX

Herausgegeben in Zusammenarbeit mit dem Moritz Verlag
von Markus Weber

Ausgezeichnet mit dem Deutschen Jugendbuchpreis

www.beltz.de
Erstmals als MINIMAX bei Beltz & Gelberg im August 2005
© 1978, 1982 Beltz & Gelberg
in der Verlagsgruppe Beltz · Weinheim Basel
Werderstraße 10, 69469 Weinheim
Alle Rechte vorbehalten
Ausgabe in englischer Sprache für die deutschsprachigen Länder
© der englischen Übersetzung bei Andersen Press Ltd., London
Gesamtherstellung: Beltz Bad Langensalza GmbH, Bad Langensalza
Printed in Germany
ISBN 978-3-407-76025-8

Once upon a time, a little bear and a little tiger
lived down by the riverside. Where you can see
smoke rising into the air, beside the big tree.
They had a boat too.

They lived in a nice little house with a chimney.

»How happy we are!« said Little Tiger.

»We have all we could wish for, and we don't have to be afraid of anything. That's because we're so strong, aren't we, Bear?«

»Yes,« said Little Bear. »I'm as strong as a bear, and you're as strong as a tiger. That should do.«

---

chimney: Schornstein

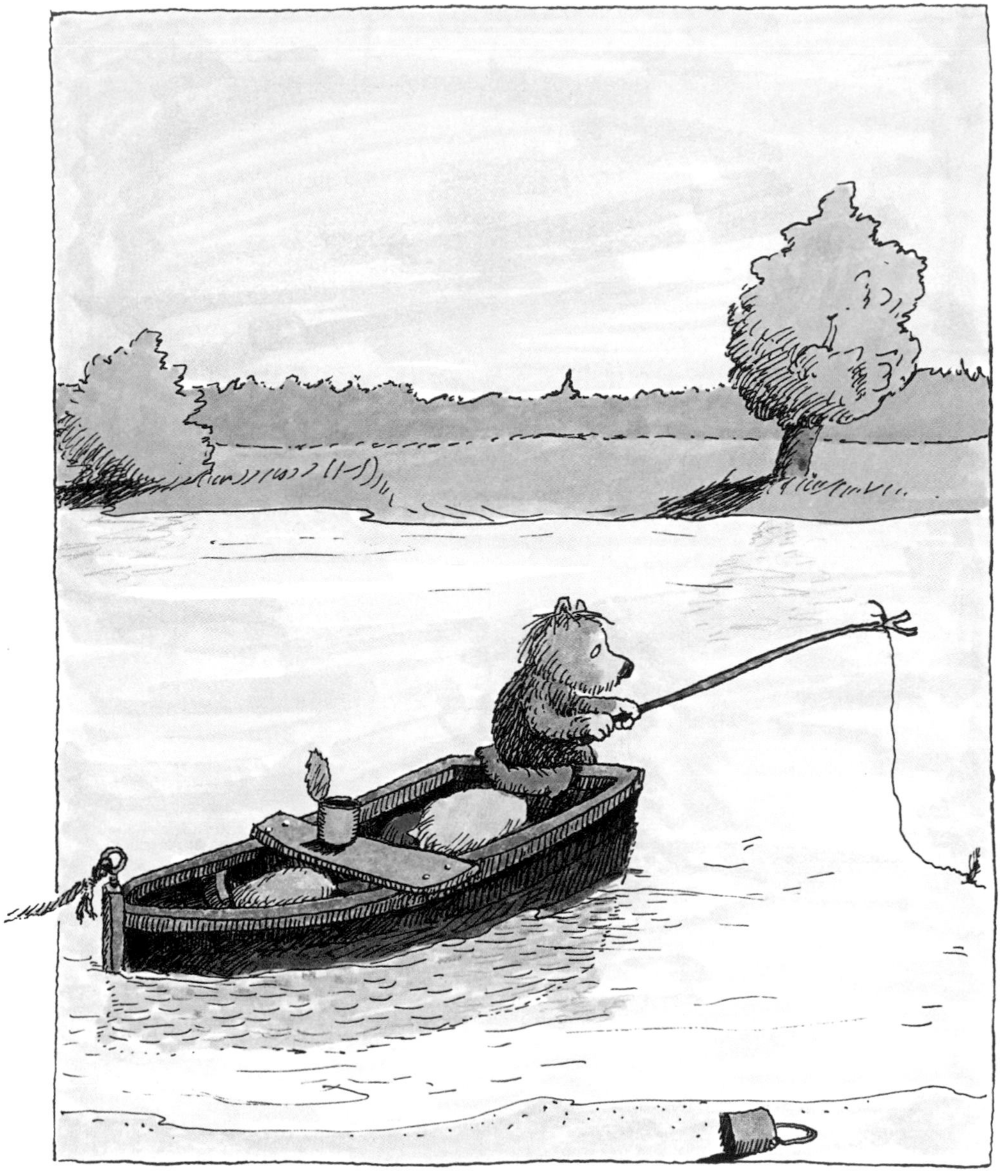

Every day, Little Bear took his rod and went fishing and Little Tiger went out in the woods looking for mushrooms.

Little Bear cooked their dinner every day, because
he was a very good cook.
»Would you rather have the fish cooked with salt
and pepper or lemon and onion, Mr Tiger?«

»All of them!« said Little Tiger. »And I want the biggest helping!«

After the fish they ate stewed mushrooms, and then they had bilberry jam and honey. They really did lead a very happy life in their nice little house down by the riverside ...

the biggest helping: die größte Portion
bilberry jam: Heidelbeermarmelade

Until one day a crate came floating down the river.
Little Bear fished it out of the water, sniffed it, and
said, »Oooh … bananas!«

---

crate: Kiste

The crate did smell of bananas. And what was that
word written on it?

»Pa-na-ma,« read Little Bear. »This crate comes
from Panama, and Panama smells of bananas!
Oh, Panama is the land of my dreams!«
He ran home and told Little Tiger. He went on
talking about Panama far into the night.

»Everything is much nicer in Panama, you know,«
he said. »Panama smells of bananas all over.
Panama is the land of our dreams, Tiger. We must
start for Panama first thing tomorrow, mustn't we,
Tiger?«
»First thing tomorrow,« agreed Little Tiger.
»Because we don't have to be afraid of anything,
do we, Bear? But we must take my stripy tiger
duck with us.«
Next morning they got up much earlier than usual.
»If you don't know your way,« said Little Bear,
»the first thing you need is a signpost.«
And he made a signpost out of the crate..

signpost: Wegweiser

»We must take my fishing rod too, because if you
have a rod you can always catch fish, and if you
can catch fish you needn't go hungry … «
»And if you needn't go hungry,« said Little Tiger,
»there's nothing to be afraid of, is there, Bear?«
Little Tiger took the red cooking pot too.

»So that you can cook me a nice dinner every day, Bear! Everything you cook tastes so good. Yum, yum … «

Little Bear took his black hat as well, and then they set off, going the way the signpost pointed. They walked along the river bank.

Just a minute, Little Bear and Little Tiger!
Don't you see that letter in a bottle floating down
the river? It might be a secret message about
pirates' treasure! Too late. It's floated past now.
Soon they met a mouse digging a hole.

»Hullo, Mouse,« said Little Bear. »We're going
to Panama. Panama is the land of our dreams.
Everything is different there. Much bigger … «
»Bigger than my mousehole?« asked the mouse.
»Impossible!«
Well, how can you expect mice to know anything
about Panama?

They passed an old fox, who was just having a
goose for his birthday treat.

»Which is the way to Panama?« asked Little Bear.

»Turn left,« said the fox, without giving the matter
much thought, because he didn't want to be
disturbed. Left was the wrong way; they shouldn't
really have asked the fox.

birthday treat: Geburtstagsfeier

Then they met a cow.

»Which is the way to Panama?« asked Little Bear.

»Turn left,« said the cow. »If you turn right you get to the farmhouse, and I'm sure the farmhouse can't be in Panama.«

Left was the wrong way again. If you keep on turning left, where do you get to in the end?

Yes, quite correct!

It soon started to rain. Big raindrops kept falling from the sky.

»I'm not afraid of anything so long as my stripy
tiger duck doesn't get wet,« said Little Tiger.
Where is your beautiful umbrella, Little Bear and
Little Tiger? You left it at home, hanging on the
door.
That evening Little Bear built them a shelter from
the rain, out of two old oil drums.

shelter: Schutzhütte

They lit a fire and got warm.

»How nice it is to have a friend who can built a shelter from the rain,« said Little Tiger. »With a friend like that, you don't have to be afraid of anything.«

When it had stopped raining they went on.
Soon they felt hungry, and Little Bear said,
»I've got my rod, so I'll go fishing. You wait under
this big tree, Tiger, and light a little fire so we can
cook our fish.«
But there wasn't any river, and if there isn't any
river a fishing rod is no use.

Luckily Little Tiger was good at finding mushrooms, or they might have gone hungry after all.

»If you have a friend who can find mushrooms,« said Little Bear, »you don't have to be afraid of anything, do you, Tiger?«

Soon they met two people carrying their harvest home, a hare and a hedgehog.

harvest: Ernte

»Come home with us, do!« said the kind hare and hedgehog. »You can stay the night. We like having visitors who can tell a good story.«

Little Bear and Little Tiger sat on a lovely comfortable sofa. »This sofa is the most beautiful thing in the world!« said Little Tiger. »We'll buy ourselves a sofa like this when we get to Panama, Bear, and then we shall have everything we could wish for, shan't we?«

»Yes,« said Little Bear.
Then Little Bear told the hare and the hedgehog about Panama. He talked about Panama all evening.
»Panama is the land of our dreams,« he said.
»Panama smells of bananas all over, doesn't it, Tiger?«
»We've never been beyond the far end of our field,« said the hare. »Our field has always been the land of our dreams, because it grows the corn we eat. But now the land of our dreams is Panama! Oh, Panama is so wonderful!«

Little Bear and Little Tiger slept on the beautiful sofa, and they all four dreamt of Panama that night.

Next day they met a crow.

»Birds are clever,« said Little Bear, so he asked her the way.

»What way?« asked the crow. »There are hundreds and thousands of ways you could go!«

»The way to the land of our dreams,« said Little Bear. »Everything is different there. Much bigger and more beautiful … «

»Oh, I can show you the land of your dreams!« said the crow (for birds really are clever). »Just fly after me. Up we go!«

And she flew up to the lowest branch of the big
tree. She flew higher and higher. Little Bear and
Little Tiger couldn't fly, so they had to climb.
»Don't let go of me, Bear!« cried Little Tiger.
»My tiger duck might break a wheel.«
»There you are,« said the crow. »That's it.«
And she pointed to the country all around them
with her wing.

»Oh, how beautiful!« cried Little Tiger.
»Isn't it beautiful, Bear?«

»It's the most beautiful thing I've ever seen,« said
Little Bear.

But all they were really seeing was the countryside and the river where they used to live before. You can see their little house, over there among the trees. Only this was the first time they had ever seen it from so high up.

»It's Panama!« said Little Tiger. »Come on, we must hurry up! We must reach that river, and build ourselves a nice little house with a chimney. There's nothing to be afraid of, Bear!«

And they climbed down the tree. Soon they came to the river. But where is your boat, Little Bear and Little Tiger? You left it by your little house, down by the riverside.

»You look for some bits of wood and planks,« said Little Bear, and he built a raft.

---

raft: Floß

»How nice it is to have a friend who can build rafts!« said Little Tiger. »With a friend like that, you don't have to be afraid of anything.«

They dragged their raft into the river and floated over to the other bank on it.

»Go carefully, Bear,« said Little Tiger. »I don't want my tiger duck to capsize. She isn't a very strong swimmer.«
When they reached the other side of the river they walked along the bank. »Just follow me,« said Little Bear. »I know the way!«

»Then there's nothing to be afraid of,« said Little Tiger, and they went on until they came to a little bridge.

to capsize: kentern

Little Bear had once built that bridge himself; by now they were quite near the bushes where their own house stood. But they did not recognize the bridge, because as time went by the river had damaged it.

»We must mend this bridge,« said Little Tiger. »You push the plank from underneath, and I'll pull it from on top. But mind my tiger duck doesn't roll into the water, because she isn't a very strong swimmer.«

Look, Little Bear and Little Tiger! There goes another bottle floating down the river. There might be a secret message inside it.

---

to mend: reparieren

Wouldn't you be interested in real pirates' treasure
in the Mediterranean Sea? Too late. The bottle has
floated past.

On the other side of the river they found a signpost. It had fallen over and was lying in the grass.

»What do you see there, Tiger?«

»Where?«

»Here, of course!«

»A signpost.«

»And what do you see written on it?«

»Nothing. I can't read.«

»Pa … «

»Paraguay.«

»No, stupid! Pa-na-ma. Panama. Tiger, we're in Panama. The land of our dreams! Oh, come along, let's dance for joy!«

And they danced for joy, in and out and round about.

But of course, you know what that signpost was, don't you? Exactly!

When they had gone a little farther, they came to a tumbledown little house with a chimney.

tumbledown: verfallen

»Oh, Tiger!« cried Little Bear. »You have good sharp eyes … tell me what you see!«

»A house, Bear. A lovely, wonderful, beautiful house. With a chimney. The most beautiful house in the world, Bear. We could stay and live there, couldn't we?«

»And it's so nice and quiet, Tiger,« said Little Bear. »Just listen!«

Their old house was rather weatherbeaten, what with the wind and the rain, so they did not recognize it. The trees and bushes had grown taller, so everything was a little bigger.

»Everything is much bigger here, Bear,« cried Little Tiger. »Don't you think Panama is a beautiful place?«

They started mending their house. Little Bear built a roof and a table and two chairs and two beds.

»The first thing I need is a rocking chair,« said Little Tiger, »or I won't be able to sit and rock myself.«

And he made a rocking chair.

---

to recognize: wiedererkennen
weatherbeaten: verwittert

Then they planted things in the garden, and soon everything was just as good as it used to be. Little Bear went fishing, and Little Tiger went looking for mushrooms. In fact, it was even *better* than it used to be, because they bought themselves a soft, plushy sofa. Then they thought their little house among the bushes was the most beautiful place in the whole world.

»Oh, Tiger,« Little Bear said every day. »How glad I am we came to Panama! Aren't you glad, too?«

---

a plushy sofa: ein Sofa aus Plüsch

»Yes, I am,« said Little Tiger. »Panama is the land of our dreams. And we can stay here for ever and ever.«

You think they might just as well have stayed at home all the time?
You think they needn't have taken a trip to Panama at all?
You're wrong. Because then they would never have met the fox and the crow.
They would never have met the hedgehog and the hare. And they would never have found out how comfortable a lovely, soft, plushy sofa can be.